STILL MORE

Night
Frights

STILL MORE

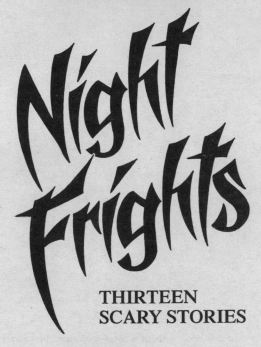

Night Frights

THIRTEEN
SCARY STORIES

J.B. Stamper

AN
APPLE
PAPERBACK

SCHOLASTIC INC.
New York Toronto London Auckland Sydney

No part of this publication may be reproduced in whole or in part, or stored in a retrieval system, or transmitted in any form or by any means, electronic, mechanical, photocopying, recording, or otherwise, without written permission of the publisher. For information regarding permission, write to Scholastic Inc., 555 Broadway, New York, NY 10012.

ISBN 0-590-62406-7

12 11 10 9 8 7 6 5 4 3 2   7 8 9/9 0 1 2/0

Printed in the U.S.A.   40

First Scholastic printing, September 1996

Contents

The Club

Have you ever moved to a new town where you had no friends? If you have, you'll know what it was like for Julio. He felt lonely. Bored. Desperate. He was so desperate that he almost joined the club. . . .

Julio was going into the last grade of middle school the year he moved to Los Padres. It was a tough time to move. Everyone was trying to be cool, and nobody seemed to have room in their group of friends for a quiet new kid. Julio spent a lot of time walking the streets of the town, hoping someone might start up a conversation. Nobody ever did.

Home wasn't so great, either. Julio's father worked late hours in a town that was over an hour away. His mother was so busy fixing up the house that she didn't have time for him. His older sister holed up in her room and listened to music. Julio started taking longer and longer walks, even after it got dark.

One night, he heard someone call out to him, someone who sounded friendly. It happened just as he was passing by the old town cemetery.

"Hey, we saw you walking by here last night. Who are you?"

Julio stopped short and looked into the cemetery. He saw three guys about his age sitting on a group of tombstones.

Julio walked closer to the low cemetery wall to get a better look at the three boys.

"I'm Julio Sanchez. I just moved into town last month."

"Hi, I'm Jim," said the boy who had called out. "And these are my friends Wiley and Tom. Why don't you come in and talk for a while?"

Julio looked into the dark graveyard and then turned around to look up and down the street. It didn't seem safe to walk into a cemetery at night. But these guys seemed friendly. And he was really lonely. Without hesitating anymore, Julio swung his legs over the low stone wall and walked into the graveyard.

"You can sit there," Jim said, pointing to a tombstone that faced his. "We were just having a meeting of our club."

"We meet here just about every night," Wiley added.

"Well, I don't want to interrupt or anything," Julio said.

"No problem," Tom said. "Hang around for a while."

"Okay, thanks," Julio said. His eyes were slowly adjusting to the dim light in the graveyard, and he tried to make out the faces of the three boys sitting in front of him. He could see their eyes clearly, but it was too dark to tell what they really looked like. Probably he'd never recognize them if he saw them on the street in the daylight.

"So, how do you like living here?" Jim asked.

"Kind of boring," Julio said. "I haven't gotten to know many kids yet."

"I remember what that was like," Wiley said. "Life can be a real drag."

"We three are lucky we got together," Tom added. "It gets pretty lonely hanging around by yourself."

"So does your club have a name or anything?" Julio asked.

"We call it the Cemetery Club," Jim said with a laugh. "Not very original, huh?"

"Sounds kind of original to me," Julio said. "Why do you meet here?" He felt really relaxed with these three guys, but it still seemed kind of weird that they were all hanging out in a graveyard.

"It's close to home," Wiley said. "Anyway,

3

what's wrong with it? Does this place give you the creeps or something?"

Julio looked around at the rows of tombstones sitting like little white houses in the cemetery. He'd never thought of cemeteries as being anything else but creepy. But being here with friends made it feel different. Quiet . . . and peaceful.

"No, it doesn't really bother me," Julio said, trying to sound brave. "But aren't there bats and other scary things around?" He was almost going to mention ghosts, but he was afraid the three friends would laugh at him.

"Hey, the things in a graveyard aren't any more scary than what you'll meet out on the street," Jim said. "Ever think of it that way?"

"No," Julio answered with a nervous laugh. "And you guys are a lot nicer than anyone I've met on the street."

"Well, maybe you can join our club," Tom said. "If you really want to, that is."

"Yeah, I think I might like to do that," Julio answered. "When's the next meeting?"

"Tomorrow night, same time, same place," Jim said. "But you can't be a real member of the club without going through . . . like an initiation. And you have to be really sure you want to join."

"Take twenty-four hours to think it over," Wiley

said. "And come back tomorrow night to give us your answer."

The three boys had suddenly gotten up from their tombstones and were fading back into the dark shadows of the cemetery.

"Okay, I will," Julio called after them. "Tomorrow night. Same time. Same place."

He didn't know if Jim, Wiley, and Tom heard him, because they had disappeared into the cemetery. Julio felt the cold marble of the tombstone underneath him, and suddenly a chill shot through his body. He jumped up and ran over to the stone wall of the cemetery. He crossed it with a leap and ran down the street toward home. All the way there, he thought about the club.

The next night, Julio walked toward the cemetery with a smile on his face. He'd made up his mind. He was going to join. Jim, Wiley, and Tom were the only kids in the new town who'd paid any attention to him so far. And they'd probably be in the middle school when classes started again in a few weeks. It would be great to have three friends you knew you could count on.

Julio came up to the place in the cemetery where he had met the boys the night before. He peered into the shadowy graveyard, but no one was there. Then it suddenly hit him. They had just been making fun of him last night. There really wasn't any club. And the next time he saw Jim, Wiley, and Tom, they would tease him for believing them.

Julio turned away from the cemetery and looked up the lonely street toward home.

"Hey, Julio, you came," Jim's voice called out from the cemetery.

Julio whirled around and saw the three boys sitting on the same tombstones. He couldn't believe that they hadn't been there a minute ago.

"We thought you might not show," Wiley said. "Not everybody is ready to be a member of the Cemetery Club."

"Well, I am," Julio said, jumping over the fence. He walked over and sat down on the same tombstone he had sat on the night before.

"Okay, then, let's start walking," Jim said.

The three boys were off their tombstones and moving through the cemetery before Julio could ask any questions. He caught up with them as they slipped between the graves and climbed a steep hill that rose to the top of the graveyard.

Julio struggled along behind them, barely keeping up. Even though they didn't seem to have any trouble, he was getting caught by bramble bushes and tripping over low tombstones. And the hill was much steeper than it had looked from the street. By the time he reached the top, where Jim,

Wiley, and Tom were waiting, Julio was short of breath and sweating . . . from exhaustion and from a sense of fear that had been slowly creeping over him.

"Okay, this is the place," Jim said, pointing down into the darkness in front of them.

Julio suddenly realized where they were standing. The steep hill in the cemetery was really one side of a high cliff that overlooked the town. For a minute, a wave of dizziness came over him. He grabbed out for Jim's arm, but he just caught air.

"Are you all right?" Wiley asked. "You still want to go through with it, don't you?"

"We really want you to be part of the club," Tom said.

"It's tough at first," Jim added. "But then you're with friends . . . forever."

Julio gulped. Suddenly he was afraid. But he didn't want to chicken out. This really was the only chance he had to make friends.

"So what do I do?" he asked.

"Jump," Jim said.

A pang of fear shot through Julio's body. "I can't do that," he said.

"Do you want to be a member of the club or not?" Jim asked.

Julio looked at the three boys in the moonlight. He wasn't so sure anymore. They looked different now. And scarier. Their eyes were sunken into

their faces. And their bodies seemed so thin —
almost like skeletons.

A shudder of fear traveled through Julio's body.
Suddenly, he understood.

"You said you wanted to join the club," Wiley
said.

"And to be a ghost," Jim added, "first you have
to die."

"N-o-o-o-o!" Julio screamed as he ran past them
and back down the hill. He ran and ran until he
was out of the graveyard.

He stopped only once to look back. There, in the
cemetery, he saw Jim, Wiley, and Tom sitting on
their tombstones. Then, just like ghosts, they disappeared.

Audrey

In the beginning, I was as mean to Audrey as the rest of the kids were. She was new in school, but it wasn't just her newness that made her different. Audrey was so different that she might as well have been from another planet.

Her parents made her wear skirts or dresses all the time. And they were so long and dowdy that Audrey looked like an old woman. Her face was different, too. No makeup, of course. But it was more than just that. Her eyes were deep brown, with darkish circles under them. Her mouth was always set in a thin line, and she never laughed. Her brown hair hung to her shoulders without a curl or curve. And she wore a corny necklace all the time, a locket in the shape of a heart with an initial A carved on it. That was Audrey.

There was one more thing about Audrey. She wanted to be my friend more than anything in the world.

"Go away!" my friends would say to Audrey when she first started following us around. They all knew that Audrey wanted to be with me. It was obvious because she always tried to sit beside me in class, and she always volunteered to be my partner for projects. I was kind of embarrassed by her attention. I wondered what I had done to make her so loyal to me.

After a while, Audrey got the hint when my friends closed her out of our circle. But I think she knew that I always understood how she felt. Because I couldn't be mean to her. Somewhere inside me, I knew what Audrey was feeling. It was weird in a way . . . almost as though we were twins separated at birth, but I was the pretty, popular one and she was the dull, ordinary one.

By the end of October, Audrey had pretty much stopped following me around. My friends all made jokes about having gotten rid of her. So they were really surprised when I made out the list for my annual Halloween party. Audrey was on it.

"Are you crazy?" my best friend, Amanda, said. "Finally you get rid of that parasite, and now you invite her to your party. It's going to start all over again — she'll try to sit with you at lunch, she'll call you after school, she'll be pestering all of us."

"It's not going to hurt anybody if Audrey is at the party," I said, feeling a little embarrassed.

"There's going to be forty people there. Audrey won't get in anybody's way."

"You just feel guilty," my friend Diane accused me. "But if you invite her to the party, she'll just start wanting to be with you again. Then we'll all have to be mean again, and you'll end up feeling even more guilty."

I didn't listen to what any of them said. The next day at school I handed Audrey her invitation to the party. I watched as she opened it up and read it. Then she looked up at me and smiled the most beautiful smile I had ever seen. It lit up her whole face.

"Thank you," Audrey said. "I'll be there, no matter what."

"Great," I said. "It's a costume party, you know. Starts at seven-thirty . . ." I sort of trailed off because I didn't know what else to say. I almost apologized for how my friends had treated her. But Audrey looked so happy that finally I just smiled back and then walked away.

On Halloween night I was so nervous that I just about jumped out of my skin when my brother dangled a rubber spider in my face. I loved giving parties, but I worried about every little thing — the decorations, the food, how my parents would act — until the first guest arrived. Then I relaxed and enjoyed myself.

The first person to arrive that night was Amanda. She was dressed as a hippie from the sixties, and even I didn't recognize her right away.

"Far out," I said, looking at her costume. Then the doorbell rang again, and a flood of people started to arrive.

Kara came as a flapper, Emily was a cat, Gwen was Peter Pan, Jim was a mummy, Andrew was Frankenstein. Within fifteen minutes, the house was filled with my friends all in funny and strange costumes, all shrieking with laughter and having a great time.

I rushed around, trying to make sure that everybody had enough to eat. But in the back of my mind, something was nagging at me. Where was Audrey? She had sounded so happy about getting an invitation. And for some strange reason, I was really looking forward to seeing her. Had her parents stopped her from coming?

We started to bob for apples, then played a couple of games. I almost forgot about Audrey until the doorbell rang at 8:30. I rushed over to it, wondering if it might be her or some trick-or-treaters. I opened the door, and for a second, my heart stopped beating.

Audrey stood on the doorstep, staring straight into my eyes. She didn't have a costume on. In fact, she had on one of her old school dresses. The locket was hanging around her neck, as always. But there was something more frightening about Audrey than anyone else in a strange costume. It was her face. Her skin was even paler than usual. Her eyes were sunken in, and they had a haunted look that was almost desperate.

"Audrey, come in," I said. "Are you all right? You look . . . well, tired or scared."

"I wanted to come to your party so much," Audrey said. "I'd do anything to be here tonight."

I reached out to take her hand to lead her into the room, but it was so cold that I dropped it.

"I'll get you some warm cider," I said. "Sit down for a while, if you want."

Audrey curved her lips a little into a smile. Then she went and sat in a big chair in the corner of the living room. She looked happy there, all alone. I brought her the cider and then said I'd have to look in on the party.

"Thank you for asking me tonight," she said. "I'll never forget it."

Right then I got the same weird feeling that Audrey and I were twins — that we were sharing the same thoughts. But this time, I felt as though I was in another world — far, far away from the party going on around me. A chill shot through my body, and I started to shake all over. I looked into Audrey's eyes, and suddenly I got really scared.

"Hey, you're missing the party!" Amanda's voice shouted in my ear. "We need you to get more food."

I snapped out of whatever had come over me. It had been scary, and this time I couldn't wait to get away from Audrey.

"She looks like a ghost, even without a costume," Amanda whispered in my ear. "What were you thinking, asking her here tonight?"

"I don't know," I said shakily.

"Well, we all told you not to ask her. Now she'll always be haunting you."

Throughout the night, while I was having a good time with everyone else, I'd look over to that chair in the corner and see Audrey. She'd be looking back at me with her deep, dark eyes, and then she'd smile. It seemed as the night went on that her smile became weaker and weaker. Then, at about 11:45, I saw her get up from her chair and start to walk to the door.

She seemed to know that I would follow her.

"Thanks for coming, Audrey," I said as we reached the door. "I'm sorry I couldn't spend more time with you."

"You asked me to come," she answered. "That's what's important. And I'll always be your friend. Always."

A big lump rose in my throat. I didn't know what to say to her. I was touched, but I was

14

scared, too. Then she reached around her neck and undid the clasp to her locket. A minute later, I felt her cold, cold fingers around my neck. She fastened the clasp of the locket at the back of my neck and then looked down at the gold heart with the A on it hanging below my face.

"Never take it off," she said. "So you'll never forget me."

Before I could say anything, Audrey was out the door. It was almost as though she had disappeared. I realized that my knees were shaking and my heart was pounding. I turned around and walked back to the party. But I didn't have any more fun that night. I couldn't forget Audrey.

The next morning in school, Ms. Sloan, our homeroom teacher, told us the news. Audrey wouldn't be with the class anymore. She was killed by a hit-and-run driver the night before at 7:30. Her parents had refused to let her go to a Halloween party. She had run away and tried to get there by herself.

Everyone in the class who had been at my party gasped and turned to stare at me. I reached up and clutched the gold locket around my neck.

And I knew Audrey was right. I would never forget her.

The Ring

An icy shiver cut down Benjamin's spine. He had two miles to walk through the cold February air. And the storm from the night before had made the sides of the road soggy and dangerous. Worst of all, he was late.

In half an hour, he was due at Ellen's house. They were making plans for their wedding, and she had warned him not to be late. Her parents were already disappointed by her choice of a future husband. Benjamin was so poor that he hadn't been able to buy Ellen a diamond engagement ring. On her left hand she wore only the narrow gold band that his grandmother had willed him. It would have to do as a wedding band as well.

Benjamin checked his watch and saw that he was getting later by the minute. As he came up to the old town graveyard, he remembered that there was a shortcut through it to Ellen's side of town. He looked at the narrow stone path that wound through the cemetery. It looked no worse than the muddy sides of the road that he had been walking on. And no cars would come along to splash him.

Benjamin gazed up at the darkening sky, filled with heavy gray clouds. Bare tree branches lashed above him, as though they were angry at the weather. He pulled his coat collar up tighter around his neck and struck off down the path.

In the middle of the cemetery, there was a hollow that Benjamin had forgotten about. As he looked down into it, he saw that the path was covered with water there. There was no time to turn back, he decided. He'd have to push on and walk around the hollow through the old tombstones. At least Ellen's house lay directly on the other side of the graveyard where the path led.

Benjamin looked up at the sky again, his face etched with worry. He didn't like being in the cemetery at night. But if he hurried, he would make it out just before the light faded completely. He began to thread his way through the old tombstones, noticing that many were over a hundred years old. The storm had knocked some of them over, and the ground was even soggier than the sides of the road.

Benjamin looked up to see how far he had to circle around before he made it back to the path.

When he looked down again, he saw something at his feet that made his breath choke back in his throat.

The storm had washed away the dirt from one of the gravesites, and lying on the cold wet ground in front of him was a skeleton. The tombstone at its head had fallen over and sunk into the muddy ground. Benjamin could see the rotted remains of a wooden coffin underneath the skeleton. But what caught his eye in the dim twilight was the ring. It sparkled even in the gloom of this stormy night.

For a few minutes, Benjamin froze in his footsteps. The sight of the skeleton had frightened him. But he couldn't take his eyes off the ring. It was the sort of ring he knew Ellen had dreamed about. Fate seemed to have brought him to this spot. And the skeleton's hand seemed to be reaching out to him, offering him the ring.

On trembling knees, Benjamin reached down and felt the tips of the skeleton's fingers. Immediately, he shrank back from their cold touch. But the ring beckoned him. He couldn't turn his eyes away from it.

Again, Benjamin reached out for the bony hand. This time, he forced himself to pick it up. Then he reached out to slip off the ring. Suddenly, the skeleton's fingers seemed to curl down and dig into his hand. Benjamin jumped back with a scream and dropped the hand. He looked away from the skeleton to the inky blue sky. What was he doing? He shouldn't waste any more time. He should just get out of the cemetery.

But the ring drew him toward it like an obsession. He wanted it for Ellen. Once more, he bent down and picked up the hand. It felt freezing cold, but Benjamin didn't let himself think. He jerked the ring off the bony finger, thrust it in his pocket, and then started to run. By the time he reached the edge of the graveyard, his heart was pounding like a frightened animal's. He wasn't sure if he was happy that he had taken the ring or not.

His feelings changed a half hour later when he slipped the ring onto Ellen's finger. She looked at him with glowing eyes and seemed to believe his story that he had been saving for the ring and only now could afford it. Even her parents treated him better. They all sat together making final plans for the wedding. It would take place the following week. And Ellen would be wearing her diamond engagement ring to the altar.

The night before the wedding, Ellen kissed Benjamin good night at her door, thanking him again for the beautiful ring. All week she had been wearing it proudly, showing it off to her friends and relatives. But she had told no one about the dreams she was having. The dreams troubled her sleep and gave her headaches during the day. She decided that they were just part of the nervousness she felt about the wedding. But the dreams were disturbing. And terrifying.

Ellen went up to her bedroom and got ready for her last night alone. She noticed that, as on other nights, the ring seemed to get colder on her finger as it got later. Shivering, she put on her warmest nightgown and crawled under the thick blankets on her bed. For a long time, she tossed and turned. She wanted to go to sleep, but she was afraid of the dreams. She didn't want them to come again.

And the ring. It was getting so cold on her finger again. Just like the other nights. The coldness stole through her bones and drained away her body's warmth. The diamond itself felt like a piece of ice. Ellen wanted to slip the ring off her finger, but she knew that was wrong. It might mean bad luck for her marriage the next day.

Ellen lay in bed shivering. Suddenly she heard a sound that made her freeze into stillness. It was the clicking sound of bones in her room. Her beautiful ring seemed to burn her flesh with its coldness.

Then a voice cut through the darkness.

"I've come for my ring."

"No," Ellen whimpered. "I don't have your ring, only mine."

The bones rattled nearer to her bed. Ellen felt a freezing draft of air sweep over her.

"I've come for my ring," the voice said again.

Ellen tried to hide deeper in her covers. The ring was so cold on her hand that her fingers had turned to ice. The bones clicked and clacked and rattled nearer.

The voice was hovering just over her head. "I've come for my ring," it breathed down on her.

Benjamin stood by the altar in the church the next morning. As the music of the wedding march began, he turned around and saw his bride. She was coming toward him down the aisle. Her beautiful dress trailed after her. Her face was covered by a lace veil. And the diamond ring sparked on her gloved hand.

All the fear and nervousness that Benjamin had been feeling fell away at that moment. He watched his beautiful bride as she slowly walked toward him and joined him at the altar.

The minister began the service. The music, the vows, the sermon — they all went by quickly. Then the moment came when Benjamin and Ellen were pronounced husband and wife.

"You may kiss the bride," the minister said, smiling at Benjamin.

Benjamin turned to his bride. He took her gloved hand with the ring sparkling on it in his.

The hand was cold, and so thin. Then he reached out with his other hand and pulled up the bride's veil.

And as he bent to kiss her, he saw her face — the grinning, bony face of the skeleton, staring back at him.

Poltergeist

Mariah had always had a wild imagination. So when she moved with her family into an old house in a new town, they didn't take everything she said seriously. At first. But after a while, they couldn't ignore what was happening.

Mariah's bedroom was on the second floor, just at the top of a curving flight of stairs. The very first night she slept there, a strange thing happened. She was lying under her sheets and blanket, almost dozing off to sleep. Then, suddenly, the covers were jerked down to the bottom of the bed.

Mariah lay there, shivering and screaming at the top of her lungs. Her parents ran into the room, wondering what had happened.

"Something was in here," Mariah stuttered in a shaky voice. "I was lying really quiet, and all of a sudden, somebody . . . something . . . pulled my covers off."

"Now, Mariah, that's just your imagination at work," her father said. "You probably kicked them off yourself while you were having a dream."

"No," Mariah whimpered. "It really happened. I heard a sound on the stairway right afterwards. Something is haunting this house."

Mariah's parents soothed her to sleep, but they didn't pay much attention to her story. Until the next evening.

The family was sitting around the fireplace reading after dinner. Mariah was reading a book about ghosts, her eyes getting wider by the minute. Suddenly a weird noise, almost like a mad laugh, came out of the fireplace. Then chunks of soot fell down the chimney, sending a cloud of black smoke into the room. As Mariah and her mother and father jumped up, coughing and choking from the smoke, another laughing sound echoed from the chimney.

"I know what it is," Mariah said. "It's a poltergeist, a mean kind of ghost that likes to play tricks and scare people. I just read about them. And I think one lives here."

Mariah's father didn't say anything. But he quickly doused the fire and shut the vent to the chimney. Whatever might be up there, he didn't want it to come down into the house.

The poltergeist left the family alone for a whole week. Mariah's parents decided that her idea

24

about the house being haunted was nonsense after all. They tried to find other explanations for what had happened with the fireplace. It must have been a squirrel, they said.

Then the poltergeist struck again.

Late one night, there was a knock on the front door. Mariah's father walked down the stairway to open it. But no one stood on the doorstep outside — no one at all. Mariah's father shook his head and walked back up the stairs. As soon as he reached the top, the knocking started once more on the front door. He walked down again and opened the door. No one was there. But out of the darkness came a mad laugh, and the door slammed shut in his face.

Mariah had woken up and seen what happened. She saw the look of fear on her father's face as he climbed back up the staircase. With shaking knees, she crawled back into her own bed, pulled the covers up over her head, and held onto them tightly.

All was quiet. Then a tapping started on Mariah's window. At first it was so quiet that she thought it must be a tree branch blown by the wind. Slowly, the tapping grew louder and louder until it sounded like a desperate animal trying to get into her room.

Mariah tried to scream, but nothing came out of her mouth. She huddled under her covers, afraid to look at what might be outside the window. Then, suddenly, the tapping was inside her room. It started on her closet door, sounding like someone was inside trying to get out. Then it traveled around the room, along the walls, until it came to her bed.

TAP. TAP. TAP. RAP. RAP. RAP. The sound pounded into Mariah's brain. Soon it was only inches above her head. She screamed.

It was the loudest, longest scream her parents had ever heard. They rushed into her bedroom to find Mariah sitting straight up in her bed, her face pale and sweating.

Together they heard the mad laugh of the poltergeist fade away outside the window.

Mariah refused to sleep in her room anymore. Her parents couldn't bring themselves to argue with her. The poltergeist had gotten to them, too.

The next morning at breakfast, the family decided that they would have to move. No matter how much they liked their new house, they couldn't share it with the wicked poltergeist.

It took Mariah and her parents three days to pack up all the things they had moved into the house. But instead of being sad, they all felt happy that they were escaping. Mariah caught herself singing as she filled boxes with her books and clothes.

The moving van arrived on a Friday and loaded

up the family's belongings. That night, Mariah slept in a sleeping bag in her parents' bedroom. Every once in a while, she thought she heard strange sounds outside the window and up and down the stairway. But she just squeezed her eyes shut hard and told herself that after tonight, she'd never be bothered by the poltergeist again.

The next morning, the family had their last breakfast in the house and loaded their bags into their station wagon. Mariah sat in the backseat and turned around to look at the house one last time as her father drove down the lane. She raised her hand in a wave to the house and whispered, "Good riddance, you mean old poltergeist."

As she turned around to look at the road, a familiar, haunting laugh rose from behind her. Mariah heard the poltergeist's voice whisper in her ear.

"Where are we going?" it asked.

Horrorscope

Dana woke up that morning from a bad dream. For a second, she remembered what horror had jolted her from sleep. But then it slipped and slithered back into the dark sleep world of her mind. She lay in bed for several minutes, almost paralyzed by an overwhelming feeling of fear. What terrible thing had happened in her dream? What had left her heart beating fast and her knees weak with dread?

The alarm clock blared out music suddenly, breaking her thoughts. Dana looked and saw that it was 7:00. She had to hurry to get ready for school. She was a freshman in high school, and already she was feeling stress.

"Morning, Dana," her mother murmured as she blew on her hot breakfast coffee. "How did you sleep?"

"I had a bad dream," Dana answered, getting

herself a bowl of cereal. "It was gross. But I can't remember what it was about."

"You're just being superstitious again," said Mark, her younger brother. "A dream's not going to hurt you."

"Thanks for the advice," Dana answered. "But you don't have the problems I do now that I'm in high school. I've got two exams today and tryouts for the lacrosse team. No wonder I've got bad dreams."

Mark just ignored her and picked up the morning newspaper. He propped it up in front of his face and read the front page of the sports section.

Dana spooned her cereal into her mouth, thinking of all the problems she faced at school today. If only she hadn't had that dream. It cast a shadow over the whole day. Just then, she noticed the back page of the paper Mark was reading. At the top of one column was the daily horoscope. That was sure to cheer her up, Dana thought. Horoscopes were always full of suggestions for how you should act to make the day better.

"Let me have the back of the paper, Mark," Dana asked, reaching over for it. "I want to read the horoscope."

"Oh, come on, you don't believe in that stupid stuff," Mark mumbled from behind the paper. He made no effort to hand her the back section.

Dana shot a glance at her mother. Her mother sighed and then said to Mark in a stern voice, "Mark, share the paper with your sister."

Dana gave her brother a smirk as he handed over the back section that included the horoscope. Then she ran her eyes down to the listing she was looking for.

**SCORPIO: Bad luck will stalk you today.
Beware FHS 422.**

A strange feeling swept over Dana as she read the horoscope. It was a feeling like déjà vu, when you sense you've experienced exactly the same thing before. But this wasn't déjà vu — it was a powerful sense of evil and fear.

"Dana, what's wrong? You're almost white. And you're trembling!" Her mother's voice drifted through her mind as though it were a hundred miles away.

Then there was a crash, and Dana felt a sharp pain in her right hand. She looked down to see blood oozing out of a cut on her palm. The table was a mess, full of broken glass from the milk pitcher.

"Mark, you clean up the table," her mother ordered. "Dana, let me put a Band-Aid on that. I can't believe you're so clumsy — even now that you're in FHS."

Dana winced when she heard her mother say the initials for Fairview High School. They had been in the horoscope. And following FHS was today's date — April 22, 4/22.

"I don't think I should go to school today, Mom," Dana said. "Something bad might happen."

"Nonsense, Dana. You know you have those two exams. You studied for them all last night. And what about lacrosse tryouts? You can't miss that. This cut isn't so bad."

"Okay, Mom," Dana said, knowing it was no use arguing with her mother.

"Now hurry upstairs, get your books, and start off for school," her mother said.

Dana ran upstairs to brush her teeth and comb her hair. She picked up a small hand mirror to look at the back of her head. But as she did, a wave of dizziness came over her. She lurched against the sink and tried to catch herself. The sound of the mirror cracking snapped her back to reality.

Mark looked in from the hallway.

"Seven years bad luck," he sneered. "You'd better be careful today, Dana. You're breaking everything in sight."

Dana stared down at the shards of broken glass from the mirror. Bad luck was stalking her today. And, suddenly, she was sure she shouldn't go to school.

"Dana, I'm sending you straight out the door to

school right now," her mother said as she put her arm around Dana and guided her out of the bathroom. "Now you get your books and start walking before you're late. I've got to get to work myself."

Dana grabbed her books from her room and followed her mother's directions. Mark ran ahead of her down the stairs and sprinted out the front door toward Fairview Middle School.

" 'Bye, Mom," Dana called out as she shut the front door behind her.

"Good luck on your exams and lacrosse tryouts," her mom called after her. "Tell me all about it when we get home tonight."

Dana forced her feet to walk one step at a time down the street toward the high school. Already, she couldn't remember the formulas she had memorized for the algebra test. And the lines from the poem that she was supposed to recite were a blurry confusion in her mind.

"Meow!"

Dana looked up sharply. A cat was standing in front of her on the sidewalk, its back raised up and its mouth open in a hiss. It was a black cat.

Dana stopped in her tracks as the cat slowly walked across the sidewalk in front of her and disappeared through a hedge. Her heart was beating fast again, and the words of the horoscope ran through her mind like a nightmarish echo.

Bad luck will stalk you today. Beware FHS 422.

Dana turned around and started to walk in the opposite direction from the high school. She couldn't go there today. She had to get away from all the crazy things that were happening to her.

The park where she had hung out as a kid was just ahead. Dana began to run toward it. It didn't matter if she cut school today. Only bad things were going to happen there anyway.

Without looking, Dana ran across the busy street that bordered one side of the park. Then she heard a loud honking noise and the screech of tires.

Dana looked at the car that was coming toward her. There was no way she could get out of its way. Frozen in terror, she watched the fancy grill and headlights hurtle toward her. And just at the last second, she saw the car's license plate. FHS 422.

It was the last thing she ever saw.

The Other Side

Ned and Jason were the only two boys who had to stay at school over the holiday weekend. Everyone else's parents had come to rescue them from Branston Academy for Thanksgiving. Ned lived too far away for his parents to come. Jason lived closer, but he might as well have been an orphan. His parents were always traveling. Over this Thanksgiving, they were in Africa.

On Thanksgiving Day, Ned and Jason joined the headmaster's family for a turkey dinner. Mr. Palmer, the headmaster, had two daughters. One was fourteen years old, like Ned and Jason. The other was just five. Kate, the older one, sat between the two boys at dinner.

"Have you seen the ghost yet?" Kate whispered during dessert.

Jason looked at her before answering. Was she serious or kidding? He wanted to impress her, for more than one reason.

"No, not yet," he said cautiously. He raised his eyebrows at Ned, who was listening.

"What ghost?" Ned whispered back.

"The ghost of one of the boys who went to Branston Academy," Kate said. "He died at school the day after Thanksgiving. He comes back every year around the same time he died."

"You're kidding, right?" Ned said.

Just then, Mr. Palmer cleared his throat and started to talk about the history of Thanksgiving. Kate and the boys had to listen and pretend they were interested. But as soon as they got up from the table, they went back to talking about the ghost.

"I'm not kidding," Kate insisted. "I think I saw the ghost myself when I was ten. I was up in the attic of your dorm, and I felt a presence. I saw something strange move across the room."

"Show us," Jason whispered, "tomorrow night."

"Tomorrow night," Kate agreed.

"I don't believe in ghosts," Ned said as the two boys walked back to their dorm. "I think she's just trying to make fools of us."

"No way," Jason said. "She said she might have seen the ghost herself. And it's not the first time I've heard this story. My older brother went here, too, and he told me the same thing."

"Yeah, right," Ned said. "I'll believe it when I

see it. But I don't mind spending an evening with Kate, ghost or not."

The next evening, the boys waited for Kate in their dorm, an old building that had been on campus for over a hundred years. The clock struck nine. Then ten. Then eleven.

"I told you this was just a joke," Ned said. "She was kidding us."

"Shhhh, I think I hear somebody," Jason whispered.

They both listened to the footsteps coming up the creaking stairs to their second-floor room. A few minutes later, Kate was standing in the doorway.

"Ready?" she asked, her eyes dark and serious.

Jason jumped to his feet. But Ned asked, "Ready for what?"

"We're going up into the attic," Kate said. "That's where I saw the ghost."

"The door to the attic staircase is locked," Ned said. "Anyway, we're not allowed up there."

Kate pulled an old key out of her coat pocket. "I know where my dad hides it."

"Let's go," Jason said.

The two boys followed Kate to the old door. The rusty key wouldn't turn in the lock at first. But finally Kate clicked open the lock, and the door swung open.

"Follow me," she said, starting up the stairs.

Jason went next, following with his eyes the beam of Kate's flashlight as it searched the darkness.

"Creepy," Ned said as the light picked out the old rafters and dusty cobwebs.

Kate walked straight toward the center of the attic and shone the light on a table there. "It's still here," she said in an excited voice. Jason and Ned hurried to where she stood and looked down at the strange board sitting on the table.

"What is it?" Ned asked.

"A Ouija board," Kate answered, "to call spirits."

Kate sat down and put her hands on the board. Ned and Jason sat down across from each other.

"What spirits?" Ned asked.

"The spirits of the dead," Kate answered. "You know, ghosts."

Ned looked over at Jason's face. It looked strange lit up by the flashlight. Jason seemed to believe all this stuff.

Kate kept staring at the Ouija board. "This is how you do it," she said. "You put your hands on the smaller board — that's a pointer. Then you concentrate and ask a question. The Ouija board will help you communicate with the spirit you want to talk to."

"But we don't even know his name," Jason said.

"I do," Kate answered. "His name was Oliver. Oliver Schuman."

Kate shut her eyes and placed her hands on the pointer board. Jason did the same. Ned sat watching them, wondering if he was the only sane one left.

"Oliver, can you hear me?" Kate asked in a low voice.

Ned watched as the small pointer board began to move across the Ouija board. Then it stopped, pointing to YES. Just then, the light flickered. And the flashlight rolled from the table and fell with a crash to the floor.

Everyone jumped. Ned bent down to pick up the flashlight and set it back on the table. He looked at Kate and Jason. They had both closed their eyes and still had their hands on the board.

"Oliver, come back," Kate said, pressing her hands onto the pointer. "Do you like where you are now?"

Again, the pointer underneath Kate and Jason's hands began to move across the board. It stopped at NO.

Kate and Jason's eyes flew open. They looked down at the Ouija board.

"He hears us," Kate said. "He just answered from the other side."

The hair was standing up on the back of Ned's neck. But he wasn't ready to believe in ghosts. Or spirits. Or Ouija boards.

"What are you talking about?" Ned asked in an angry voice. "What other side?"

"The other world. The world of dead spirits. The world of ghosts," Kate said. "Oliver traveled back from it to talk to us."

"Put your hands on the board," Jason said, looking hard at Ned. "Come on!"

Ned reached out his hands and saw that they were trembling. Quickly, he put them down on the Ouija board. The wood was warm where Kate and Jason had touched it.

Once again, Kate started to call to the ghost of Oliver Schuman.

"Oliver, come back. Cross from the other side. Are you near us?"

Ned felt a pressure under his hands. The pointer was moving again. He wanted to take his hands away. But he couldn't seem to move them.

"I feel his presence," Kate whispered with her eyes closed.

"I do, too," Jason said.

"No," Ned said. "He can't come back. Nobody comes back from the other side."

Just then there was a rumble of thunder not far away. Heavy pellets of rain hit the roof of the old attic.

"We shouldn't be here," Ned said, scared and wanting to go. "It could be dangerous being up here in this storm."

Kate and Jason ignored him.

"Oliver, can you talk to us?" Kate said in her low voice.

There was another rumble of thunder. The rain pounded down harder.

Ned watched as the pointer began to move across the board again. It seemed to be spelling out a word.

Then, suddenly, a flash of lightning filled the sky. Ned felt pain rip through his body. He felt as though every nerve ending inside him were on fire.

Everything went black for a long, long time. Then Ned saw light all around him. He reached his hands out into what seemed to be glowing clouds. He tried to touch Jason's and Kate's hands on the Ouija board. But nothing was there, just soft emptiness.

"Ned, can you hear us?"

"Ned, come back." It was Kate and Jason calling him.

Ned tried to answer them. But his mouth made no sound.

"Ned, can you hear us?"

Ned wanted to answer. But he didn't know how. He didn't know how to get back yet.

From the other side.

Good Luck Charm

Raymond slumped down in the backseat of the car. He didn't even have to look out the window to know what they were passing. Huge, spiny cactuses. Tumbleweeds rolling in the wind. And miles after miles of desert.

"Where are we going, Dad?" Raymond's sister, Felita, asked from beside him. Then she turned to Raymond and rolled her eyes.

"Same old place," her father answered with a grunt from the driver's seat. "You'll like seeing it again."

"Right," Raymond mouthed to Felita. They were both bored with going to the old mining town. It was the only place their father wanted to drive to when he got a day off from work. They lived in an apartment building in the city. Just once, Raymond wished they could go somewhere exciting.

Their father switched on the radio and began to

hum along with the music. Raymond hunched farther down in his seat and shut his eyes. He could see the mining town in his mind. A few straggling shops. A gas station. But mostly it was a ghost town now. Nobody wanted to live there anymore. It was no wonder.

"Think you'll see that old woman again, selling things?" Felita asked.

Raymond opened his eyes and looked at her. "I don't know. But I brought my money along."

"Don't waste it on her," Felita said. "That's just old, weird stuff she has."

Raymond shut his eyes again and started to think about what the old woman had spread out on her blanket the last time they were in the town. He didn't know why, but he wanted something from her. And today, he planned on getting it.

Raymond woke up as the car jolted to a stop. Looking around, he saw that they had arrived at the old town.

"You kids can walk around," their father said, turning around. "I'm going to talk to Miguel over at the store."

Raymond and Felita watched their father walk with a springy step to the old store where his friend Miguel worked. He would talk there for two or three hours. Then they would drive home again.

"Come on, let's stretch our legs," Felita said. "I'm going to run up to the hill that looks over the town."

"Go ahead," Raymond said. "I'll roam around here." He wasn't an athlete like Felita. She took off down the empty road at a fast jog.

Raymond got out of the car and started to walk down the dusty street. Most of the buildings were vacant. The old clapboard was peeling paint. Signs dangled crookedly from rusting nails. It was a ghost town, all right. Raymond got the chills walking through it sometimes.

Raymond turned to the left down the second alley he came to. That was where she had been last time — the old woman selling carved turquoise, strange-shaped rocks she found in the desert, and other odd things. His heart beat a little faster when he saw her there, sitting in the sun with a blanket spread out in front of her.

"Hi," Raymond said as he walked up to her.

The woman turned her wrinkled face up to him and stared at him with deep brown eyes. But she didn't say anything.

Raymond squatted down on the ground and looked over the objects on the blanket. He was glad Felita wasn't along. She said the woman sold

strange things — things that were full of super-
stition.

Raymond picked up an animal's skull that had
been polished by years of being out in the desert.
He turned it over and over in his hands.

"Coyote," the woman said to him. "Full of
power. It will bring you strength."

Raymond laid the skull back down and fingered
a snake skin. It was scaly and seemed strangely
alive to his touch.

The woman reached down and picked up a
small piece of turquoise. She put it in Raymond's
palm.

"You could buy this as a gift," she said.

Raymond shook his head. He wasn't looking for
a gift. He was looking for something to carry with
him. Something that would bring him luck.

On the far corner of the blanket, he saw something he'd never noticed before. It was a rabbit's
foot. As he reached for it, the woman grabbed his
hand.

"What's wrong?" Raymond asked. "I want to
see it."

The woman seemed to hesitate. Then she let go
of Raymond's hand. He reached down and picked
up the paw, which had gray fur and small claws at
the end. It felt warm in his palm.

"How much is it?" Raymond asked.

"I can't sell it to you," the woman said. "It would be bad luck for me."

"But I want it," Raymond said.

The old woman picked up the paw and put it in Raymond's hand.

"Take it," she muttered. "But be careful."

Raymond stood up, holding the paw in one hand and stroking its fur with the other. He looked again at the woman and then ran down the alley to the main street.

His father and Miguel were sitting on the steps of the store where Miguel worked.

"What do you have there?" his father asked Raymond.

"A rabbit's foot," Raymond said, holding out the foot for them to see. "It's going to be my good luck charm."

Miguel's face screwed up when he saw the foot. "Did you get that from the old woman?" he asked.

Raymond nodded yes.

"You should throw it away, then," Miguel said. "She practices magic. That foot might still have the animal's spirit in it."

Raymond looked down at the paw. He wasn't going to throw it away. He looked at Miguel and shrugged and then walked away.

On the way back to the city in the car, Raymond turned the paw over and over in his hands.

"That's gross," Felita said. "I wouldn't carry around part of a dead animal. Anyway, maybe the animal didn't want its foot cut off. Did you ever think of that?"

Raymond looked down at the rabbit's foot. Suddenly it scared him. Maybe there was a reason the old woman had refused to take money for it. Maybe he should throw it away. But instead he pushed it down into his jeans pocket so Felita couldn't see it anymore.

Raymond started to close his eyes, but the sudden screech of the car's tires made him jump in his seat. He looked out the front window and saw a huge jackrabbit bounding across the road in front of the car. A second later, there was a loud, grinding crash, and everything went black.

"Raymond, Raymond, are you all right?"

It was Felita's voice, calling him out of the darkness that had drowned him. Raymond opened his eyes. Felita and his father were standing over him. Both of them looked very sad and very concerned. There were bright lights all around.

"What happened?" Raymond asked. "Where am I?"

"You're in a hospital," his father said. "We had an accident. It was that rabbit. It was crazy. It jumped in front of the car over and over again."

"It was so scary," Felita said, her voice shaking.

46

"It didn't leave after the wreck. Dad and I were okay. But you were lying on the ground. And the rabbit . . . it came up and pulled something out of your jeans pocket."

Raymond felt a shudder of fear travel through him. Then he looked away from their faces to the bottom of the bed. One leg was propped up and wrapped in bandages. He tried to wiggle his toes. But there was nothing to wiggle — nothing at all.

"That rabbit's foot," his father said. "You should have thrown it away. It was bad luck."

Moans from the Closet

The Wilton house was the most famous place in the old New England town. George Washington had actually slept there. The townspeople liked to brag about that. But they didn't brag about the horrible thing that had happened in the same bedroom Washington had slept in. They tried to hush that up. What weird old Mr. Wilton had done was a blotch on the house's reputation — one that just wouldn't go away.

Sam didn't like living in the small town. On long, hot summer days, there was nothing — absolutely nothing — to do. His mother had gotten bored, too, so she had volunteered to become a tour guide at the old Wilton house. The house brought a fair number of tourists into the sleepy New England town every summer. People came to see where George Washington had slept during one of the battles of the Revolutionary War. And while they were in town, they bought souvenirs, ice cream cones, food, and even watercolors from the art gallery.

Sam had liked the old Wilton house when he was little. He'd loved hearing stories about the first president sleeping there. But now he was a teenager, and George Washington didn't interest him much anymore. Nothing in the town interested him anymore.

"Why don't you come along to work with me today, Sam?" his mother asked at breakfast one morning. "Maybe you can help answer people's questions about the history of the house."

"Naw, that's okay," Sam said, his mouth half full of cereal. "That place is boring, except for the stories about old Mr. Wilton."

"You keep quiet about Mr. Wilton," Sam's mother said, her eyes flashing warning signals. "The mayor wants that whole story forgotten. Enough people still ask about him and the horrible thing he did. We want to give tours of a historic house, not a haunted one."

Sam didn't respond. He just kept eating his cereal. But in the back of his mind an idea was forming. An idea about how he could add a little excitement to the summer.

That afternoon, Sam walked over to the Wilton house, where his mother was at work.

"Come to see your mother?" asked the woman taking money at the door.

Sam nodded his head. He hated to lie, but it was the only way he could get in without paying. He knew his mother was working out in the back of the house this week, describing the house's herb garden and landscaping.

"Go ahead, then," the woman said. "We've got a good crowd today. Just don't bother any of the people who are taking the house tour."

Sam smiled to himself as he slipped through the door into the big sitting room on the ground floor. He wasn't going to bother anybody. He was just going to add a little excitement to the tour.

Sam sneaked around the edge of a group of people listening to the tour guide's lecture about the history of the house. He made a beeline for the staircase that led up to the famous bedroom. He knew that if he timed it just right, he could get there in between two tour groups.

Sam looked left and right as he reached the top of the stairs. Perfect. The tour group that had just visited the bedroom was now on its way down the servants' steps to the old kitchen. He crept quietly along the hall to the bedroom where Washington had slept.

No people were in the room. The big old four-poster bed with its blood-red comforter stood in the middle of the room. The bed had been there when Mr. Wilton had killed his wife. But it couldn't have been there when George Washington spent the night. Still, most of the furniture in the room was really old. The highboy dresser. The rocking chair where Mr. Wilton had patiently rocked, listening to his wife's moans as she slowly died in the closet.

Sam looked over at the small closet door, which was only four feet high. It wasn't really a closet — more like a storage place. He had gotten his mother to admit to him that it was where Mr. Wilton had locked up his wife. And it was where the police had found her body a month later.

Sam knew most kids would be afraid to get in that closet. But he wasn't. He didn't believe in ghosts. He just liked to make fun of people who did.

The sound of footsteps on the stairs echoed down the hallway and into the room. Sam knew he didn't have much time. He ducked under the velvet rope that kept tourists from roaming around the room and touching everything. Quickly, he pulled open the low closet door and crawled inside. It was a much smaller space than he had thought. But there was no turning back now. He crouched on the floor and pulled the door shut behind him.

Just in time. The tour guide came into the room making her presentation. She droned on about how George Washington had come to the Wilton house one stormy night during the Revolutionary

War. He had been given a warm bed in this very room. And on the small table, he had spread out his maps by candlelight and plotted his strategy for the next day's battle.

Finally, the tour guide paused and asked if anyone had questions. Two adults asked questions about the history of the house. Then Sam heard a younger voice pipe up.

"Wasn't this the room where Mr. Wilton killed his wife? Somebody told me to see the closet where he locked her up to die."

"Yeah, what about that?" another voice asked. "I hear both their ghosts haunt this place."

"I'm sorry," the guide said hastily. "We don't discuss that rumor. We're here to educate you about the house's important history."

Sam heard her footsteps start to leave the room. Other people began to follow her.

"I'll bet old Wilton stashed her in that little closet," a girl's voice said.

"I hear he laughed at her the whole time she was moaning and dying," another boy said.

"Come on, let's get out of here," the girl said. "Everyone else has gone."

Sam knew it was the perfect time. First, he let out a soft moan.

"What was that?" the girl asked.

Sam moaned again, a little louder.

"It's coming from the closet," the boy said.

"Come on, I'm scared," the girl hissed, her voice sounding panicky.

Sam listened to them run down the stairs. He laughed to himself. They probably thought it was Mrs. Wilton's ghost.

Sam tried to stretch out his legs, but the closet was too small. As he reached to open the closet door, he heard the sound of another tour guide's voice come down the hallway. Too late. He'd have to wait awhile to get out and stretch. Anyway, now he had another chance to scare somebody.

The next time he moaned from the closet, it was even better. An old lady actually started screaming. The tour guide came back up that time. He heard her walk over to the bed and probably look under it. But she didn't get near the closet. Maybe she was afraid of it, too.

The bad part was that he never got a chance to crawl out of the closet for the rest of the afternoon. And it was getting really hot in there. He couldn't move out of one position, and he was beginning to feel drowsy. So drowsy.

Sam woke up when he heard the sound of a latch sliding across the outside of the door.

"Hey," he yelled, trying to push the door open. But it didn't budge.

"Hey, let me out of here," he cried out. "I'm Sam Jarret. My mother works here."

No voice answered him from the other side of the door. There was no sound in the house at all. Sam wondered how long he had slept. Maybe all the tour guides and tourists had gone.

Then he heard the creaking sound. Creak. Creak. Creak. It was the sound of a rocker rocking back and forth, back and forth, across the old floorboards. Creak. Creak. Creak.

"Who's out there?" Sam yelled. He was beginning to feel desperate. He'd never been claustrophobic before. But this closet was getting to him.

Creak. Creak. Creak. The rocker just kept rocking.

Sam began to pound on the door. He was in a panic now. He didn't know who was out there in the room. But he knew he had to get out of the closet.

He pounded and yelled until he was exhausted. Then he stopped and listened. The creaking of the rocker had stopped, too.

Then the sound of the latch scraped against the old wood of the closet door. And, slowly, the door was pulled open.

An old man's face was staring at him, lit by the light from the candle he was holding. There was a crazed look in his eyes. Sam didn't have to ask Mr. Wilton his name. He knew.

The old man laughed and slammed the door back shut on Sam. Sam heard the latch slide shut again. And as Sam sat there in the dark, frozen in terror, he decided he believed in ghosts after all.

Meanwhile, Mr. Wilton's rocking chair creaked back and forth . . . back and forth . . . back and forth.

Too Late

Amy and I had been best friends since kinder-garten. We were always there for each other. But now all that has changed. Amy isn't the same person she used to be. It all began when the foreign exchange student came into her house. I knew from the start that he would cause something bad to happen. I tried to stop it. But I was too late.

I was sitting in my bedroom that afternoon when I got a telephone call from Amy.

"Jasmine, you've got to come over here. Now!" Amy's voice sounded breathless and a little scared.

"What's the matter?" I asked. I knew Amy exaggerated sometimes, and I was in the middle of a good book.

"He's here, the foreign exchange student my family is sponsoring. And he's so creepy. I can't stand it that he's going to be living in my house for the next three months!"

"I'll be right there," I said, and hung up the phone. I rushed out of the house and ran the four blocks over to Amy's house. When I got there, she was waiting for me on the porch.

"What's going on?" I whispered, trying to peer through one of the living room windows to see if I could see this guy who had Amy so upset.

"I told my mom that I didn't want him living here," Amy said in a trembling voice. "But she said she's made a commitment to the school. He's come all the way from Austria. We're stuck with him for three months."

"Well, if your mother thinks he's okay, maybe you're just imagining things," I said, trying to make her feel better. "Where is he?"

Just then the front door opened and a tall, thin young man walked out onto the porch. I can't really describe the feeling that came over me when I saw him. But I know that my blood started to run cold, because goose bumps rose all over my body. All around me, the air seemed to have changed and become thick and full of evil.

Amy cleared her throat uneasily and looked from me to him.

"Jasmine . . . this is Kurt Muller. Kurt, this is my friend Jasmine."

I met the cold blue eyes that seemed to be staring straight into my brain. I finally stuttered out a hello.

"Please tell your mother that I will be back for dinner, Amy," he said. "It was very nice to meet you, Jasmine." I smiled as he spoke to me in his polite, low voice. But when he smiled back, I caught my breath. His smile looked unnatural, like an animal baring his teeth.

"Do you see what I mean?" Amy hissed in my ear as Kurt walked down the sidewalk. "Isn't he creepy?"

"He's creepy, all right," I agreed. "But what are you going to do about it? Somehow you're going to have to put up with him for three months."

"Not if I can convince my mom to make him leave," Amy said. "Come inside. I want you to see his stuff."

We walked into Amy's house and bounded up the stairs. Amy and her parents slept on the second floor; Kurt had been given the third floor, which had been an old attic turned into a bedroom. Amy's older brother, who was now away at college, used to sleep there.

"Are you sure we should be doing this?" I asked as we came to the closed door to the attic bedroom.

"You've *got* to see this," Amy said as she pushed open the door. "He's not going to be back till dinner. You heard him say that."

I followed her into the low-ceilinged room, which was lit dimly by two small gable windows.

"It's over here," Amy whispered, suddenly sounding guilty. "I took a peek already when Mom drove him over to see the high school this morning."

I went over to the bureau where Amy was standing, staring at the objects that had been carefully laid out on top of it. The silver medallion hanging from a silken cord caught my eye first. I started to pick it up to study the strange inscriptions on it, but Amy caught my hand.

"Don't touch anything!" she warned. "I don't want him to suspect that I've been up here."

Beside the medallion was an old iron key, the kind you only see in movies set in old castles. And beside the key there was a thin book, bound in red leather. The writing on the cover was old-fashioned and ornate, and in a language I'd never seen before.

"What do you think it means?" I whispered.

"That's the problem," Amy said. "I have no idea. But it scares me."

I looked at her eyes that were troubled by fear, and I suddenly wanted to do anything I could to help her. I sure wouldn't want this creep staying in my house. And I didn't want him scaring my best friend, either.

"Run down to your room and get a piece of

paper and a pencil," I said. "Maybe if we can figure out what the words on this book mean, we can get your mother to get rid of him."

Amy took off down the steps, and I looked around the room some more. I opened the closet door and saw his clothes hanging there. Most of them were black — black turtlenecks and black jeans. I knew other guys who dressed like that sometimes, but not all the time.

Amy came back with the paper and pencil and I took it from her to copy down the words on the red book. It was harder than I thought. I couldn't really tell what all the letters were because the type was so strange and fancy. Just as I was finishing the last letters of the last word, a sound floated up the staircase. It was the sound of the front door opening.

I took one look at Amy's wide eyes and knew we had to get out of there fast. We tiptoed to the door and crept down the stairs to the second floor as we heard the sound of his footsteps on the stairs leading up from the entranceway. My heart was beating so hard that it hurt by the time we reached the second floor. Amy made a run for her bedroom and I followed. I turned around just as I was shutting her bedroom door behind me. He was standing in the hallway, his cold blue eyes hard and his lips drawn in a smirk. I slammed the door and sank down on the floor.

"See!" Amy whispered. "He's horrible! I'm like a prisoner in my own house."

I looked down at the strange words I'd copied onto the paper. I didn't know how I'd figure out what they meant, but I knew I had to find out.

I took the paper with the book title on it to the library the next day. I searched through dictionaries and encyclopedias, but I couldn't find anything that looked remotely like those strange letters. Finally, I asked the librarian for help.

"Where did you get these words?" she asked with a puzzled look on her face. "I believe they're in some European language, but I'm not familiar with it."

"Uh, I found them on an old book," I said, stumbling over my words. I wasn't sure I wanted to admit where I'd gotten the book title.

"Maybe you can try the library at the university," she said, "if you can find a way there."

I knew that wouldn't be any problem. My mother taught at the state university in our town. But she was away on a business trip and wouldn't be back for three days.

I called Amy with my news as soon as I got home.

"I don't know how I can wait," she said, her voice sounding panicky. "Mom thinks I'm crazy for

61

being so nervous about him. But it's so awful having him stare at me across the table at breakfast and dinner. I can't even eat anymore."

I heard Amy make a scared sound in her throat just then. She whispered into the receiver that she couldn't talk anymore and hung up. I knew why. Kurt must have come into the room. For a minute, I let myself think that Amy was just getting paranoid. But then I remembered how I'd felt around him.

The three days dragged by until my mom came home. Every day in school Amy told me stories of weird things that Kurt had done. I knew it was a long shot that the book title could tell us anything about him, but I had to find out.

Finally, Mom came home and agreed to take me to the university library. She even looked at the words I had written down, but said they didn't make any sense to her. Just before we left for the library that evening, I called Amy.

"How are you doing?" I asked in a worried voice.

"Not so good," Amy answered. "Mom has to go to a meeting tonight and Dad's away on a trip. I think I'm going to be left alone in the house . . . with him."

"Don't worry, I'll call you from the library," I said, "as soon as I find out what the book is about."

"Okay, but don't forget," Amy said shakily. "I'm counting on you."

The librarian guided me to a dusty corner of the reference room that was filled with old dictionaries in foreign languages. She pulled one from the shelf that had the same strange kind of letters on the front as the book had.

"Try this," she said. "It's a language from the old Hungarian empire. It was spoken in Transylvania years ago."

Transylvania. I couldn't remember why that sounded familiar to me. I started going through the dictionary, searching for the words. Slowly, I wrote them down, one by one.

A   Tasting   Guide   to   Human

My heart started to beat faster as I searched for the meaning of the final word. It was in the front of the dictionary. The fear that was forming in my mind grew and grew and finally came true as I found the final word.

Blood

With a cry, I jumped up and ran to the telephone. I punched in Amy's telephone number and waited with my heart pounding.

I heard the phone being picked up and a low voice answered, "Hello." It was him!

"I want to speak to Amy," I said, sounding desperate.

"She's right here," he answered, and I could see the horrible grin that must be on his face.

"Jasmine?" Amy's voice asked. To my surprise, she didn't sound scared at all.

"Amy, I found out what the book title is. You've got to get away right now."

"It's too late now," Amy said dreamily. "Too late."

She was right. I was too late. Amy lives in Transylvania with Kurt's family now. She pretends that she went over there as a foreign exchange student. But I know better.

Amy did leave me something to remember her by, though. The day she left, I found the thin red leather book in my mailbox. It was inscribed with my name. And blood type.

What a Night!

My friend Eve is a pain in the neck. Ever since she was a little kid, she's been afraid of the dark. I've tried to get out of her what happened to make her so scared. But every time I start asking questions, her mouth shuts as tight as a coffin lid.

But tonight I'm not going to take no for an answer. It's the big night of the year — the night when everybody is out. I'm not planning on sitting around like a moldy old corpse while everybody else is having fun on Halloween.

"No, I won't go!" Eve said stubbornly. She stared out the window at the dark violet sky. It was slowly deepening to a rich midnight blue.

"You've got to get over this," I said, looking into her green eyes. "If you don't face your fears, you're never going to get out and see the world." I gave her a wide smile, showing off my teeth.

"Besides, it's Halloween. Everybody is going to be out — even the little kids."

As soon as I mentioned Halloween, Eve shrank back into her favorite red velvet chair. I could tell from the look on her face that she was upset — really upset.

"Not Halloween!" she cried. "That's the worst night of all. People walk around in costumes. But underneath those costumes, you never know who they are. They might be somebody out to get you!"

"Oh, man!" I said with a sigh. It was beginning to look like another boring night hanging out in Eve's basement. I like this girl, but sometimes. . . .

Just then, I looked up through the high window in the room, and I saw a full orange moon rise over the treetops. It was so bright that it shone light down on everything like a yellow spotlight.

"Presto, no more dark!" I yelled and grabbed both of Eve's hands. I pulled her up out of the chair and pointed at the moon.

"Come on, there's nothing to be afraid of now. Old Mr. Moon will light our way."

Eve sort of whimpered like a little kid. I could tell she was still afraid. But my mood must have been catching, because a big smile slowly spread across her face, and the moonlight glinted off her beautiful teeth.

"You won't leave me alone, will you?" she asked.

"Cross my heart and hope to die," I said with a silly laugh.

Eve laughed, too, and I pulled her up the steps and out into the night.

We were dressed all in black, so it was easy to slip from shadow to shadow along the streets. We watched the kids running up to the houses, yelling, "Trick or treat!" The kids were older and bigger now that it was dark. Some of them even looked our age. So we knew no one would be suspicious if they saw us hanging around in the dark. It was so exciting that chills ran down my back. But Eve clung to my arm. She hadn't been out in so long that she was jittery.

"Come on," I whispered to Eve, "let's go up to some houses."

"No, let's just watch," Eve murmured. "I'm scared."

I decided that talking was going to get me nowhere. I grabbed Eve's hand and pulled her off down the street toward a big old house I had passed by many times at night. It had the spooky old look that I loved. I even had dreams of living there some day. I was sure it must have a really great old basement.

"Where are we going?" Eve asked.

"Just trust me," I said. "I've always wanted to

look inside this house. We'll pretend to be trick-or-treaters, and whoever lives there will have to answer the doorbell. Then I can look inside."

Eve didn't answer me, but I could tell she wasn't very happy. We passed by a couple of other teenagers on the street. When we smiled at them, they told us we had great costumes.

"Those kids were weird," Eve said. "Did you see the fake blood and tacky fangs they had on?"

"Yeah," I answered, "that blood looked disgusting."

We had gotten to the sidewalk that led up to the front door of the old house. It loomed up before us in the night, looking like the set for a horror movie. The roof was full of gables that jutted out, giving it a creepy silhouette against the night sky. The windows were dark except for one on the ground floor, where candlelight was glowing out into the night.

Eve followed behind me up the sidewalk to the door.

"Can't we just go home now?" she whispered. "I don't like this place. It gives me the creeps."

"That's what I like about it," I answered. "Just stay behind me. Nothing's going to happen to us."

I picked up the heavy iron knocker on the door and let it slam down on the old wood. Even I had to admit that it was pretty creepy. We waited for a couple of minutes. Then we heard footsteps coming toward us on the other side of the door. Heavy footsteps. A second later, the door swung open.

Everything hit us at the same time. The man's scary-looking eyes staring at us. The sight of the stake in his hand.

Eve's scream was so loud that it seemed to pierce my ears. I saw the man's eyes get even wider as he looked at her open mouth and shining teeth. Then he raised the stake toward us.

I turned around, grabbed Eve's arm, and started to run. She seemed to be frozen with fear, and I almost had to drag her down the front side-walk. I could hear the man pounding down the sidewalk behind us. I could smell the garlic hanging around his neck!

Eve finally got her strength and started to run beside me. She was panting with fear.

"It's him," she sobbed as we ran. "He tried to get me years ago. I'll never forget those eyes!"

I looked over at her and finally realized why she hadn't wanted to come out all these years. Then I turned around and saw the man running after us — fast. He had the stake raised and his eyes were glittering with hate.

"Hurry up!" I yelled, pulling Eve faster. I saw some woods ahead that I knew like the back of my hand. On the other side was the place where I lived.

We ran into the thick woods, dodging between

the trees. The man's footsteps pounded after us. We could still smell the garlic on the night air. We kept on running as fast as we could. The woods were getting thicker and thicker. But I knew how to get through them.

"Come on, we've got to get some distance ahead of him so we can make a run for it."

Eve's sobs had turned into real tears by this time, but she kept running. Finally, the sound of the footsteps got weaker and weaker. And the smell of leaves overcame the horrible smell of garlic.

We made it to the edge of the woods and began to run through the graves. The moon was still so bright that I knew he could spot us if he got out of the woods before we made it.

With one last sprint, we got to the mausoleum in the middle of the cemetery. I pulled open the heavy stone door, pushed Eve through ahead of me, and then threw down the iron latch.

Gently, I opened a coffin for Eve to climb into. I wiped away the tears that streaked her face and touched the tip of one of her fangs.

"I promise I'll never take you out on Halloween again," I said before shutting the coffin lid.

Then I jumped into my own coffin and breathed a sigh of relief.

What a night!

The Third Wish

The day was hot — so hot that heat seemed to rise up from the sidewalks in wavy lines. James walked along, wishing he had a car like his friends. Ten days ago, he had gotten his driver's license. Not that it did him any good. His mother used the family car to get to and from work. His father lived in another state. That left James on the hot streets. Walking.

James had just come back from a job interview. He wanted to get a summer job to earn money for a car. But this interview hadn't worked out. Now he was in a strange part of town full of buildings with boarded-up windows and peeling paint. And he had to watch his feet as he walked to make sure he didn't stumble over the places where tree roots had pushed up the sidewalk.

So when James heard the man's voice call him from close by, he jumped.

"Hey, you're a little nervous, aren't you?" the

man said. When he grinned, James could see that several teeth were missing.

"No, not really," James said. He stared at the man sitting on the stoop of an abandoned building. The man was wearing ragged clothes and needed a bath, but there was nothing threatening about him. James knew it was best not to act afraid. Still, his heart was beating faster, and he really wanted to run.

"You wouldn't have an extra dollar, would you?" the man asked James. "I haven't had breakfast yet, and it's getting way past lunchtime."

James shook his head no. At the same time, he stuck his hands in his pockets to check for the twenty dollars in emergency money his mother had given him that morning. But it was just that — emergency money. She expected James to give it back.

"That's too bad. I sure could use a square meal," the man said. "I've been down on my luck for a while now, ever since I came across this so-called piece of magic."

James knew he should move on, but the word *magic* had caught his curiosity. He was reading a lot of books right now about strange, mysterious happenings. He wanted to find out anything he could about magic.

"What magic?" James asked.

The man stared James straight in the eyes for

several seconds. Then he pulled something smooth and white from inside his jacket. It was a bone, perhaps a small human finger bone.

"What's magic about that?" James asked. He wanted to touch the bone in the worst way.

"Someone down on their luck gave it to me," the man said. "It's magic, all right. It grants any wish you ask for. But I understand you can only have three."

"If it's so magical, why don't you wish for some money?" James asked.

"No, I've taken two wishes. And that's enough for me," the man said. "Might you be interested in the bone?"

James shook his head no. But he couldn't stop staring at the bone, lying in the cup of the man's palm. Three wishes. He could use those, all right.

"How much do you want for it?" James finally asked.

"How much you got?" the man said.

James felt in his pocket and pulled out the twenty dollars. He held it out to the man.

"You've got a deal," the man said, snatching the bill out of James's hand. "Just a few words of advice. Think hard about what you wish for. Everything comes with a price."

James wasn't sure what the man meant. All he cared about was getting the mysterious bone. Finally the man handed it over. It felt cool and smooth in James's hand. He turned it over and over, comparing its length and shape to his own finger bone. When he looked up to ask the man more about it, the man was gone. He'd vanished.

James walked the rest of the way home, lost in thought. What wishes would he make? One thing was for sure, he planned on thinking it through.

That night, when his mother asked for the twenty dollars back, James almost wished it was back in his pocket. But he caught himself in time and told his mother that he had lost it on the way home from the job interview. The lecture he got made him think about how much he wanted to be able to get away from home.

That night in bed, James settled on his first wish. He decided he wanted a new red convertible, just like the one his friend Brian had. Brian's family was filthy rich, and Brian got whatever he wanted.

James pulled the small white bone out of his pocket and in the moonlight solemnly wished for a red convertible — all his own.

The next morning, when James came down to breakfast, his mother was standing by the phone. She looked pale and frightened. The sound of the phone ringing was what had woken James up.

"Sit down, James," his mother said. "I've got some bad news."

James sat down with a feeling of dread growing in his chest.

"Brian died last night," his mother said in a shaky voice. "He was in a car accident — a freak accident. His red convertible was hardly scratched. But he flew out of his seat . . . and he hit the concrete. He stayed alive for only a few hours after they took him to the hospital."

A chill came over James as he thought about Brian. They went way back — to first grade.

"There's one more thing," his mother said. "Brian's parents want you to have his red convertible. They said Brian always knew how much you wished you had one."

Suddenly James felt sick. He jumped up from the table and ran to his room. The white bone was lying on top of his dresser. James picked it up and threw it into the back of a drawer. He didn't want to see it anymore. Everything had its price.

James didn't drive the red convertible for almost a month. Then one morning he woke up feeling as if a spell had been lifted from him. He grabbed the keys to the car and drove around town for three hours. He passed by a lot of kids from his class. Some looked at him funny, as if they thought he shouldn't be driving Brian's car. Others waved and seemed to remember how much Brian had loved the car, too.

James enjoyed every minute that he was in the car. But he wished somebody could share it with him. Like Molly. She had been in his class since elementary school, too. Their last names started with the same letter, and their lockers were always close to each other. Molly had been going out with Jess for half a year now. And since Jess was the only good friend that James had left now, he knew Molly was off limits.

Still, James couldn't get her off his mind. One night, he accidentally came across the white bone at the back of his drawer. Turning it over and over in his hands, he wished he could go out with Molly.

James woke up the next morning from a bad dream — a nightmare. He was almost afraid to pick up the phone when it rang. But his mother had already left for work. The phone rang and rang. Finally, he picked it up.

"James?" a voice choked with tears asked. "James, it's Molly. Jess died last night. Nobody knows why. I've got to talk about it — with you."

James listened to Molly as she talked about Jess between sobs. He felt as though he had turned to stone inside. As Molly went on about how much she had loved Jess, James stared at the white bone on his dresser. Just looking at it made him sick. He reached over and threw it deep into his drawer again.

A week passed. Jess was buried in the same cemetery as Brian. And Molly began to call James every evening to talk about Jess and how much she missed him. One night, Molly asked if they could take a drive together the next day in Brian's red convertible. James hung up on her and walked over to his dresser. He took the white bone from the back of the drawer.

Sitting on his bed, James turned the bone over and over in his hand. Then he made his third wish. He wished his friends would come back again.

James finally fell asleep, but he tossed and turned from bad dreams. In the middle of the night, he woke up — certain that he had heard the front door of his house open and close again. After that, he couldn't go back to sleep. He lay still as a corpse in his bed, waiting. Then he heard the footsteps on the stairs. Footsteps that slowly but steadily came toward his room.

James got up from his bed. He was sweating and scared. The footsteps moved down the hallway, closer and closer. Then the door creaked open and the overhead light flickered on.

They had come back. Brian and Jess. They stood in his doorway like two zombies back from the dead. Brian was covered with dried blood.

Jess's face was gray and swollen. They both stared at James with eyes full of anger and revenge. They knew.

James grabbed for the magic white bone. He squeezed it in his trembling hands and wished them to be gone.

But James had run out of wishes. Forever.

Teach Him a Lesson

Sam and Simon were as different as two brothers could be. Sam was fun-loving, irresponsible, and the black sheep of the family. Simon was serious, reliable, and the apple of his mother's eye. It was no surprise that the brothers didn't like each other.

During the summer that Sam was twelve and Simon was fourteen, things got really bad. The boys' father had to travel for a month on business, and they were left at home alone with their mother, whose nerves quickly unraveled.

"That Sam is driving me crazy," she muttered as she peered out the window, watching for Sam to come home. "Here it is, after dark already. He knows that his curfew is before dark. And he's late again — just like last night. That boy just doesn't obey!"

Simon sat quietly in the room, rearranging the books on the bookshelf so that they were all in perfect alphabetical order by author. As he listened to his mother, he decided that it was time to teach Sam a lesson.

That night Simon devised a plan. He knew Sam was probably out hanging around town with his friends, up to no good. And to get home he'd have to walk along the dark lane that passed by the cemetery.

"Tonight," Simon thought aloud, "something will happen on Sam's walk home. Tonight I'll teach him a lesson he'll never forget."

Simon had never gone out after dark before, not alone. But he was determined that Sam wouldn't get away with what he was doing. After all, it wasn't fair that Simon should be so good and Sam be so bad.

Simon pulled the bottom white sheet off his bed and stuffed it under his arm. He had his plan all figured out. But he had to hurry.

The moon was just a thin sliver in the dark summer sky. Simon ran along the empty lane toward town. It was only a mile between their house and the town. Halfway between was the old cemetery, bordered by a stone fence.

When Simon reached the cemetery, he was already out of breath. His heart was pounding from the exercise he seldom got, and he could hear his breath coming in short pants. Looking out over the white tombstones in the pale moonlight made his heart beat even faster.

"You've got to teach him a lesson," Simon muttered to himself, partly to screw up his courage to the sticking point.

He scrambled across the low stone wall beside the lane and set his feet down in the cemetery. To his disgust, the ground was soft and seemed to sink beneath his shoes. Quickly, Simon walked toward a tombstone that was in the second row back from the lane. It was just high enough for him to be seen on it from the lane and wide enough to give him a comfortable seat.

There was a scuttling sound in the bushes by the tombstone as Simon walked up to it. His heart jumped into his throat, and for a moment he thought about running home. Running was out of the question, though. His legs were too weak from fear to move.

Finally, Simon forced himself to walk up to the tombstone and climb on top of it. He knew Sam would be walking by soon, and he intended to scare the living daylights out of him.

Simon wrapped the sheet around himself, leaving a narrow opening by his eyes. With icy fingers of fear tingling up and down his spine, he sat and waited for Sam to walk down the lane.

He didn't have to wait long. Sam came strolling down the lane, kicking a stone in front of him. He was humming a tune under his breath, as happy-go-lucky as he could be.

"I'll change his tune," Simon whispered to himself. He let out a low moan that floated across the cemetery on the summer air.

Simon watched with pleasure as Sam stopped short in the lane. Again, he let out a ghostly moan.

Slowly, Sam walked forward along the lane.

"Is that you again?" he called out into the graveyard.

For a minute, Simon stopped moaning, trying to figure out what his brother meant. Just nonsense, he decided, and let out another moan.

Sam walked a little nearer to where Simon was sitting on the tombstone. He peered straight into the cemetery, which was dark except for the pale moon that was shining off Simon's white sheet.

"Two ghosts tonight," Sam said with a nervous laugh. "There was only one of you last night."

The moan he was about to make caught in Simon's throat. He followed Sam's stare behind him in the graveyard. Sitting there, only two tombstones away, was a strange white figure. Its eyes stared back at Simon with a haunting, angry look.

Simon's scream echoed across the whole graveyard. He jumped up from his tombstone, threw off his sheet, and ran to the stone fence. As he leaped over it, he almost knocked Sam down.

"That should teach you a lesson," Sam yelled after him. "Never sit in a graveyard after dark!"

Trick or Treat

We always go out trick-or-treating together — me, my friend Jordan, Jordan's little sister Tessie, and Ruby, my next-door neighbor. There is no other day of the year that the four of us hang out together. But every Halloween, we meet at the corner by my house just when the sun is starting to sink in the sky. Over the years, we've gotten to know who is the bravest, the fastest, and the greediest. Ruby is always the greediest by far. She can never get enough treats.

So I guess you could really blame her for what happened.

This past year, I dressed up in a vampire costume that included fangs and fake blood. Jordan was a pirate, and Tessie was a little black cat. Ruby had on her old witch's costume, which was getting a little worn out. The peak of her black hat was bent over at the top, and her black witch wig was looking really weird.

We ran up and down the streets, ringing doorbells, screaming "Trick or treat!" and stuffing candy and sweets into our bags. By the time we had covered most of the neighborhood, it was dark. And we were at the farthest point away from our houses.

"I want to go home," Tessie started to whine. She always got tired first, but this year she had lasted longer than usual.

"I guess we've about covered every place anyway," Jordan said. He looked worried that Tessie was going to make a fuss.

Ruby was poking around in her treat bag, looking for her favorite kind of candy bar.

"We're not stopping yet," she said. "I've got less candy than I did last year. Every year we should get more than the last. That's my rule." Ruby talked in a way that made it hard to argue with her. We all started to walk in the opposite direction from home, not sure where we were going.

"We don't know this neighborhood," Jordan said after we'd gone about half a block. "Anyway, that old witch's house is around here."

I heard Tessie whimper a little. I could tell she was starting to get scared of the dark. I wasn't feeling too comfortable myself in the strange neighborhood.

"Look, there it is."

Ruby stopped suddenly and pointed her finger toward a house that was set far back from the sidewalk. We could see candles flickering in the two front windows, but bushes and trees hid most of the house.

I felt Tessie move closer between me and Jordan. "Does a witch really live here?" she asked.

" 'Course she's not really a witch," Jordan said. "Everybody just calls her that."

"Listen, Ruby," I said, looking around at the deserted sidewalk, "let's just go on home. There aren't any other kids trick-or-treating on this block. You can have some of my candy if you haven't got enough yourself."

"No, I want to go up to this house," Ruby insisted. "I'm not afraid of the old lady who lives here."

Ruby pushed open the low iron gate that separated the yard from the sidewalk and started to walk up the brick path that led to the house.

I looked at Jordan and shrugged my shoulders. It was too late to talk Ruby out of doing it. And we'd never live it down if we were too scared to go up with her.

"Come on, Tessie," I said, taking her hand. "There's nothing to be scared about."

Tessie sniffled a little bit, but followed us as we walked behind Ruby to the house.

"I wonder what she'll look like?" Jordan whispered.

"Long yellow teeth," Ruby whispered back. "A big hook nose. Black hair down her back."

Tessie really started to cry then. Jordan had to pick her up and carry her the rest of the way to the porch.

We stood on the porch in front of the door and waited after Ruby knocked. Nobody came. Ruby knocked again. The candles were still flickering in the windows, but the rest of the house was dark.

Then, all of a sudden, a light went on inside, and the door opened wide. We were blinded by the light for a few seconds. Then we saw the old woman standing in the doorway. She had her gray hair put up in a neat bun. Her eyes were blue, her nose was normal, and her smile was kind and inviting. Best of all was the tray of candy, cookies, and other goodies that she held in her hands.

"Trick or treat," we all said, sort of nervously.

Ruby reached her hand out to grab some of the candy off the tray, but the woman stepped back into the room before Ruby could take any.

"Come in," the woman said in a soft, sweet voice. "So few children knock on my door anymore. And I just love to welcome trick-or-treaters into my house. Let me see your costumes."

I followed Ruby and Jordan and Tessie into the house, even though my mother had given me a strict lecture never to go inside anyone's house on Halloween. But I felt silly to worry about this old lady. She couldn't be a witch. Never in a million years. She looked like the nicest grandmother in the world.

"Now, let's see, you're a pirate," the woman said, looking at each of our costumes, "and you're a cat. You're a vampire, and you," she paused as she looked at Ruby, "you're a witch."

I thought I heard her voice get a little harder and colder when she said the last word. But before I could think about it, she was offering us the tray of candy and goodies.

Ruby took two pieces of candy and a little bag of cookies and stuffed them into her bag. We all helped ourselves, and the woman just smiled and offered us more.

Ruby picked up a piece of licorice and started to bite off the end.

"No, no," the woman said sharply. "Don't eat anything in the house. Wait until you reach the sidewalk outside the gate."

Ruby lowered the licorice from her mouth and stared at it hungrily.

"But take the rest of the candy," the woman said with a smile. "Put it in your bags. I'm sure you'll be my last trick-or-treaters of the night."

So we took it all, stuffing our bags with every shape and size of candy until they were heavy.

"Happy Halloween, dearies," the old woman said as we filed out the door. "And remember, don't eat anything until you go through the gate."

Ruby was walking first down the brick path, and she was still carrying the piece of licorice. I saw the greedy look in her eyes as she stared at it. We were still on the path when she put it up to her mouth.

"Ruby, don't eat it," I said.

Ruby wouldn't listen. She put the licorice in her mouth. Suddenly she started to scream. She stood there in the moonlight screaming and screaming. The rest of us saw the licorice twist and turn in her hand. Then Ruby threw it down on the ground. We watched in horror as a snake raised its head and hissed at Ruby. Then it slithered off into the night.

Finally, Ruby stopped screaming, only to start again when the bag of candy in her other hand started to twist and turn. When she dropped it, it hit the brick path with a funny, squishy sound. We all jumped back as the bag flopped away into the bushes.

"Drop your bags!" I screamed to everyone as I felt mine begin to squirm in my hands. We all threw the bags into the grass and bushes and watched as they wiggled and squirmed away.

Ruby was the first one through the gate. We all ran after her down the sidewalk. We ran and ran. But we couldn't escape from the witch's evil, cackling laugh. It followed us all the way home.